ANTHONY SHAPLAND is a Welsh writer, artist and founder of g39, an artist-led space in Cardiff. His short story 'Foolscap' was shortlisted for the Rhys Davies Award and he has written for the BBC Radio 4 Short Works series. He has recently published *Lan Stâr*, a Welsh-language adaptation of *A Room Above a Shop*, his debut.

'A miniature world in exquisite miniature, rich with tenderness and pain. Shapland writes with such care and precision. You can only love this book' Tom Bullough

'Like looking into a kaleidoscope, every tiny twist in Anthony Shapland's novel results in a cascade of new colour and light... *A Room Above a Shop* is a story to savour, from a writer in total command of his powers' Mike Parker

'An achingly intimate story, rich and ragged with emotion, told with loving intricacy and delicate precision, *A Room Above a Shop* is vivid and embodied' Megan Barker

'An atmospheric portrayal of gay, working-class life in a South Wales Valley, to read *A Room Above a Shop* is to feel held within the hands of a master craftsman in control of his form' Joshua Jones

'One of the most beautiful and original gay novels I have read in a long time. Spare, sad and intensely poetic, like a *Swimming in the Dark* for grown-ups' Neil Blackmore

'There's a moving uncertainty, a vulnerability on the page that allows the reader to hear, and to listen. There's a quiet, brave strength in that' Cynan Jones

'Writing so vital you can feel the blood beat between the words, and the breath in the white space around them. *A Room Above a Shop* is an extraordinary evocation of love, and of life in South Wales in the years following the miners' strike' Francesca Reece

'A taut, poetic and profoundly moving tale of love. Written with restraint and care, *A Room Above a Shop* marks the arrival of a distinctive and compelling literary voice' Noel O'Regan

'A tender portrait of a love story not often heard. Shapland's writing is intensely poetic, chapters unfurl like precious flowers. Joyful and painful all at once' Hanan Issa

'An essential new voice in Welsh literature. Anthony Shapland is a beautiful writer' Tiffany Murray

'A perfect novel . . . full of beauty, tenderness, love; a true gift. Don't miss out' *Buzz Magazine*

'[An] utterly unique experience . . . This is a book of deep importance to Wales' hidden histories' *Nation.Cymru*

'A vital new voice in Welsh literature'
BBC Radio Wales Arts Show

'Beautifully blends art and fiction to find words capable of expressing the rush of clandestine love and desire, but also fear, between two men . . . A lyrical and quietly devastating debut' *Service 95*

'A lyrical, tender study of two men falling in love... Heartbreaking' *New Welsh Review*

A Room Above a Shop

Anthony Shapland

GRANTA

Granta Publications, 12 Addison Avenue, London W11 4QR

First published in Great Britain by Granta Books, 2025
This paperback edition published by Granta Books, 2026

Copyright © 2025 by Anthony Shapland

Anthony Shapland has asserted his moral right under the Copyright,
Designs and Patents Act, 1988, to be identified as the author of this work.

A version of the chapter 'Foolscap' appeared as a short story in
Cree: The Rhys Davies Short Story Award Anthology (Parthian, 2022).

Early versions of the chapters 'Doubt' and 'Split Level'
appear under the titles 'The Story of B' and 'Psychic Healing'
in the piece 'Meantime' in *Cymru & I* (Seren Press, 2023).

This is a work of fiction. Names, characters, places, and
incidents either are the product of the author's imagination
or are used fictitiously. Any resemblance to actual persons,
living or dead, events, or locales is entirely coincidental.

All rights reserved. This book is copyright material and must not be copied,
reproduced, transferred, distributed, leased, licensed or publicly performed
or used in any way except as specifically permitted in writing by the publisher,
as allowed under the terms and conditions under which it was purchased or as
strictly permitted by applicable copyright law. Any unauthorised distribution or
use of this text may be a direct infringement of the author's and publisher's rights,
and those responsible may be liable in law accordingly. Please note that
no part of this book maybe used or reproduced in any manner for the
purpose of training artificial intelligence technologies or systems.

A CIP catalogue record for this book is available from the British Library.

3 5 7 9 10 8 6 4 2

ISBN 978 1 80351 162 7 (paperback)
ISBN 978 1 80351 161 0 (ebook)

Typeset in Warnock Pro by Iram Allam
Printed and bound by CPI Group (UK) Ltd, Croydon, CR0 4YY

The manufacturer's authorised representative in the EU for product safety is BGC
Sustainability & Compliance, 7 avenue du Général Leclerc, 75014 Paris, France
(gpsr@baldwinglobalconsulting.com)

www.granta.com

For T

Foolscap

Like a beacon, the summit catches the early sun.

B stares at it from the dim kitchen. Drowsy and nervous. The kettle clicks, rolls of steam fog the window. Excitement hums through his body like a soundwave.

He packs and unpacks a bag. Leftover food from the uncounted, leftover days at the year's end. Gold-wrapped chocolates spill across the counter, toffees that cloy on gums and pull fillings.

This house is council new-ish; new enough to feel temporary. A fitted kitchen, fitted bedrooms, fitted carpets, but ill-fitting doors with weightless cardboard interiors and hollow aluminium handles. They spring click in damp corridors and close with soft cushions of air. All on one level. Accessible. Grab-handy handles and wipe-down surfaces and the smell of Dad's ashtrays and mince, which lingers even after all these months.

A cul-de-sac of plasterboard-thin units with interlocked brick driveways on an indifferent hill.

In the bath, B scrubs himself all over, again and again. Carbolic froth ebbs and ripples. A leg dangled over the edge cools as he lifts his hips to wash below. As he sinks, liquid rises in his ears and sound changes, his body an island in the milky water.

The coming expedition feels parallel to his life here, separate, unreal. It hangs just below the surface of his mind, a confusion of fear and excitement. He's not quite sure what he's walking towards. A pulling and a pushing – his instinct says go; his anxiety says stay. Either choice feels wrong. He can't not act. He can't stop the buzz, the vibration, the hunger.

They had talked at the bar a few days back. B knew him, knew who he was. Good-natured M, from Joneses, the ironmongers. Handy, knows his stock, knows his decorating kit. He was buying a round for loyal customers. A large round. All smiles and Christmas. Hands reach, spills, and drinks passed over shoulders in odd-shaped glasses, and tonic, and snacks gripped in clenched jaws and have you got a straw? Four straws, ice and a slice, and two more pints, and one for the barman and good cheer and broad laughter. Sorry. Are you waiting? Here, let me get yours. And he did.

With drinks delivered, the shopkeeper stood apart. His dark beard frothed with beer, a mid-distance stare. Then a shift, a slight difference in his posture. Or a change in his face. Maybe just a pause. He looked sad. No, not sad, just alone. B recognised something, and just like that, he cheers-ed him. B never does that.

They stood together, between tables staked out with handbags and coats. Small talk. Christmas. Doing anything? Family? Quiet one. Same.

B bought him a drink back, Christmas, after all.

Night's end, tinsel gaudy and rasping, a festive singalong. One for the road. He was drunk. They were both drunk. M pulled a sheet of foolscap from a pad above the payphone. A time and date, about a week away, written out twice then torn. One half each.

I go every single year, before the new year, up to the stone – the highest point, *Carn Bugail*, the shepherd's rock – shop's shut, see—

M's hot breath warmed his ear, the click of wet, his voice raised above the chorus.

It's an amazing view—

The music ended, suddenly.

Flushed faces flinched in the electric spark and gutter. A collective *aww* in an abrupt strip-light glare. Pints gulped. Shouts, laughter and off-key songs echoing into the street. Coats, party hats. Bodies steamed in the cold air.

B had woken the following day fogged and dry-mouthed, the yellow lined paper still in his hand. Momentarily he couldn't recall what it was. Slurred handwriting, a torn edge: *31st noon, '87.* His half of an agreement.

He remembers the smiling face that held a fleeting look he recognised well.

As he clears an arc in the mirror, he pauses in his own gaze. He dislikes shaving, but dabs some abandoned Brut 33 over his stubbly chin. He coughs. Too much, it's overpowering. He scrubs it off, his cheeks too pink, too shiny.

Held in the palm of the valley below, a freezing fog flows. Winter pale, the slope beyond is gridded with larch.

The lowland has been left to sour. Compacted new-build clay, a brownfield slicked in frost above the river and road, railway and town. The air is chill and he shudders. The valley is shrinking. Houses fall apart, worthless. A place of industry now sagging, underfed, starved of purpose. Drainage ditches choke with briars that scratch across the pasture. Flag iris fan, winter-dry and brown where reeds clump. Marginals thrive in the lost farm's soggy decline and grass cedes to scrub, white with hoar.

At least the climb will be warm, he tells himself. He pulls a red peaked cap low and hunches against the cold.

On the shallow incline the ground cracks, bog-soft and glazed with ice. It sucks and pulls. His legs swing an awkward pendulum, boots mud-heavy clod.

Behind the town the hill rises, grown from mining spoil, load by load. It's an unnatural mound poured from above, like sand funnelled through a slow hourglass. It grew until it settled, leaning back on the hollowed east mountain behind, an uneasy, weighty twin. The land held with trees in fear of slip.

B ducks into the forest and his step slows. Everything feels motionless, prop-like, scenery thrown up in haste. A man-made plantation on a man-made mountain.

A jay swoops low, bounces, and takes alarm up to the canopy. Lines of trees open and close with a pulse of shadow as he walks. Light filters onto deep slow-dropped layers of needles that make for a quieter tread. Roots reach tree to tree, binding the slope, and gusts take high branches in pulls and sways, rocking the dense floor. He's aware of the bird's silent side-eye high above, the sweep of boughs that whisper in scrapes and sighs.

He closes his eyes.

This hill is a bright map of his childhood. A play track for stunt bikes, a den, a place to be lost, to disappear with siblings. Or away from them. A place to loiter and mitch dull school days out until the bell. A place to be alone with this feeling that he's different to the others.

How often has he stared into the mirror at this hidden him? An understudy, carefully learning lines and behaviours; waiting in the wings to take the stage. Trying to understand how it is to be in this small town, a boy in this world.

He sings quietly to this other self that walks alongside him, any song he knows. Lyrics escape his memory and whistling fills the gaps where words fail. Unembarrassed, his choir-learnt bassy-baritone sounds out, clear but sad. He tries falsetto until it makes him smile, then notes flatten into melancholy.

With eyes closed he's less alone, his own footsteps come back to him. He pauses; the other him pauses. He moves through the vertical planes of trees with himself in parallel, obscured by columns of soft-split bark.

Ahead, toward the clearing, he can see the tips of larch, amber and fiery. His pace is steady.

His song stops. Sounds that had bowed soft vibrations in foliage now play staccato and sharp as the tree line ends. The light is brighter and he stands, blinking, at the edge of desolation. No longer the warm, acidic compress of forest carpet, he's surrounded by cleared trunks and scrub and a dry smell. A diesel smell. The forest cull – fire breakers, rows stripped and replanted methodically.

The wreckage is silver, bony and torn. Branches and trees have been clipped and stacked by machinery. Tyre ruts cut the path in a difficult camber. Here is the tipping point of the mine-spoil, the spout where the ground turns inside out, the moving mountain. Black and shimmering and unstable.

Stumbling, he's suddenly tired.

The days that led him here were eased by the hangover, then nervy excitement. It felt far off, possible. Now he is ambushed by hesitancy, a judder of confusion. He wonders if he's being a fool.

He sits, sinks back, down into the slope. It's cold and damp and he lies low, out of sight. A buzzard circles overhead. He pictures it slowing mid-air, wings back, before plummeting toward him, snatching his pathetic body up from the grass.

What the hell is he thinking?

He shudders. He knows only too well what he's doing out here. He wants to pay attention to the bearded man with curled hairs at his collar, who smiled.

He gets up. His throat tenses in a grip that augurs tears, or nausea. He understands the stir in his gut; why he washed so attentively; why he's wearing his good clothes, new clothes with labels that rub. He'll go to hell for what he wants, but still he climbs.

And there he is. The shopkeeper, M, in the distance.

The spring of grass and moss is kinder, the air keen, the ground softer. Sheep tracks wrap the slope like ribbons, and wool with pink and blue smit marks tufts the gorse. Early bracken curl-bright fiddleheads through grey earth. The light is clear. He feels his shoulders ease, his lungs open. The day is past the shortest, drawing out, the big sky makes it feel endless.

B's shadow walks ahead of him toward M, who squints into the bright sun as they both cross the plateau. Cold-bitten pink cheeks like his own, a gloved hand waves. They pause and their breathing slows. They walk toward each other and to the platform of rock at the highest point.

Hesitant steps. B knows how to be with his brothers, with friends, how he used to be with Dad. Men with men, mates. He understands how to behave, what to talk of, how far apart to sit.

Here at the top, they are strangers together, as on a train, limbs and bodies settle on the rock, close but distinct.

The buzzard's silent circling soothes as their eyes follow the spiral and fall of its search. B glances sideways, the shopkeeper's face is near. A drip shivers under his nose at the top of a dark moustache. His green eyes shine with wind tears.

Two breaths meet in a single drifting vapour and they sit and look out over the hills.

Few words. More gestures than chat. They both remember they've brought food, the crackle of foil, a sandwich teased in two. Squashed mince pies and a shared thermos of tea which spatters away from lips in the breeze.

The conversation eases with the sharing. The land ahead maps out their stories of relatives and memories and school. The sway of the telling and the rhythm of sounds settle between them. They talk in roundabout ways, circling a centre like the buzzard's spiral.

They find common ground. Step forward and back in words and codes and invitations and pauses. They run out of the things they can say easily, but the silence is comfortable. Side by side, they face south and talk to the hills.

The sun is overhead. Ears blush cold, sparks light hazel eyes.

A crumb of pastry is lost in his dark beard.

Their shadows get shorter,

two parallel lines.

Equal.

West

Equal.

Mirrored.

A lone cloud idles.

From the sky the buzzard marks two figures on the hill among hills. The highest point, capped by a red dot.

M takes a toffee, cold, hard and sugary. He jaws a sweet-chewed figure of eight. Speech is stuck on the horizon. He rolls the yellow cellophane square in his hand. Unrolls it. The sun drifts west and a light wind lifts.

He feels the weight of the bottles of stout in his bag, a gift from a shop customer. He forgot an opener, sorry, but offers them. B upturns one on the other. A satisfying deft twist, *pssth*, bottlecaps lift.

They clink, a cold swig sinks warm. Tart after sweet.

Chat, unstopped, pours in drink. They talk about building things, farms, pit closures and hasty, propped-up factories. Their ambitions. Blushing red as his cap, B confesses that he wants to be a painter, to learn how. He swings muddy feet. Pictures, proper like. Decorating's a step in the right direction, he reckons.

They lean in, gossip about the village, about the shop and work. Under the peak of his cap, B's brow lowers as he speaks of the strike. The anger, the divisions. His brothers' picketing, his parents adrift. They raise a solemn *cheers* in respect of their newly formed dead dad club.

B talks about wanting to leave, to see more. He feels trapped without a real job, without a trade. The river, the road and the railway run the same route. He plucks blades of grass. It feels small here. Everybody belongs to someone else. Nothing changes. A sigh in clouded breath.

Fingers shred the bottle label and he talks slowly, his cap hides his face. His throat is taut, his voice catches. A careful balance. B steps forward on each word.

Something needs to change. His jaw-tight clench pulses where his cap sits. He doesn't feel like he belongs, he loves his brothers and his sister, but feels like he'll never fit. Their arms brush. B turns, as though a question has been asked. His breath closer than the cool air.

M seeks words to offer in response, but the right ones don't come. He tries to nudge a sentence into life, some meaningful sign of understanding. He wants, more than anything, to talk for longer but, as soon as the thought arrives, he's an actor left without a script.

He looks inward to something he can't speak aloud. Something he rolls toward in countless night grunts. An imagined climax, forbidden, hidden behind locked toilet doors, under heavy blankets that pin down the deed. The hunger for another body, for a person to know, to see what he knows, to share.

He's filled with guilt. What is he doing up here? He feels caught out, seen doing something he ought not.

Sadness sinks through him in an obscure confusion of fear and shame. The heavy impossibility of the shop, of the valley below—

He blurts out that he should get home to his daughter.

A mouth opens to reply. Then swallows the sentence.

Why did he say that? His daughter lives with her mother and her stepfather, a real father to her, a better father than the grieving boy-dad he had cut. And now she's become his alibi. He feels disgusted at himself, at his life. A shopkeeper, sad and alone. A cold claws through the stone in shivers.

I don't have a daughter; I mean I do have a daughter. She's great. But she's not at home. It's just me. Just me for years. And a cat. Tigr. No *e*.

He falters.

Sorry.

They sit and stare at the ground as if something important has just been lost.

A long wait.

They peer down into the valley in pause.

B lifts his red cap and nudges the shopkeeper—

Daughter? Dark horse—

Ease returns like a clear note in a song. A glance and their shared deep broad smile. A look, unwavering, ending in a nod. Settled.

They stand. Long-sat legs are stiff and slow. Their goodbye is sincere. A hand rests on a shoulder. M feels big and clumsy, shy, an animal learning to be wild again after long performing tricks.

They walk backwards, without turning away. B waves, his red cap raised, sunlight on his open face, a smile. The new thread connecting them thrums as they start to move apart. Sinking below the east horizon, he shouts, hands cupped, mute, until the word glides into M's listening ear—

thanks.

Happy new year, the shopkeeper calls and starts his own walk west.

Step

M steadies himself for the first steps over the edge. This stretch is steep. His feet find muddy footholds worn in sod, pockets in roots and rocks and wiry grass. He's on his heels, leaning back. Legs walk ahead of his body and knees jar in the sharp descent.

With muscles more used to standing at the counter he tips forward in careful baby steps. Childish, childlike, a man of his age. A grown man. He gasps, grabs a tree and hugs tight, an anchor. The slope rolls him into a trot, a run he can't stop, even faster, skimming stones.

He wants to leap high and yell out all the things he didn't say. How he hasn't felt like this before, he doesn't know what it is, but it isn't wrong. Then gravity tips, turns, and the hill shrugs.

A skid, a slip. His bum bounces, slides, until a pile of leaves slows him to a stop. Winded, he feels drunker than he should and smiles. In his mind an image lingers, of the sun behind B, hair caught like fire. A halo, red light through ears, a shy wave – *thanks*, on a breeze. Light as air, toward home.

His head rests against earth, with beetles and worms. His tongue tastes crumbs in his beard. He looks up at bare branches bathed in sun, his chest rises and falls, puffs clouds that catch the rosy light.

A small ridged sphere uncurls on his shoulder. A woodlouse, navigating this new obstacle to sink back under cover.

Lichen furs oak and birch. Evening light glows. He lies still and breathes in the soft silent bed-warm rot of winter. Roots fix deep in the soil, reach through streams and fissures to hold on to the unmined rock below. Whatever happens next, it is a good thing.

Breathing stills, and he sits up. He knows this place. His hands crawl into the leaves. Fingernails scrape the ground.

They foraged here, before everything changed. It fed his father's fondness for anything free, his mother's despair at the grocer's wilting offerings. He wonders at the memory of her, wild mushrooms in her skirt apron, slim dirty fingers in earth.

His mouth waters at crab-apple bullets made sweet; the sherbet flowers and dark berries of the elder, the Judas tree; papery hazelnuts in the paws of thieving squirrels; wimberries stuffed in pint bottles, and remembers their stained lips with sticky, smiling teeth.

Pink

The bell of the shop door rings out to the evening. M throws the bolt and stands a moment in silence. In the window, *New Year Sale!* signs are lit by the pulse of coloured fairy lights.

In this slow disco, he takes his boots off, peels muddy jeans from damp legs, and drops them to the shop floor. He smells aftershave, not his, on his cord jacket. Keen, cheap and musky. His stomach jumps with excitement.

He wonders how close they dare go.

Through flyscreen ribbons he pads up the narrow stairs, holding a square of yellow cellophane and his half-scrap of foolscap.

He strips and washes, dropping his head to the basin to get the dirt from his hair and face. Water clouds pink. A cold-weather nosebleed runs over his top lip into his mouth.

Plugs of toilet roll stopper the iron tang of salty blood. His father swore blind that stout causes nosebleeds. He feels a wave of love and smiles in contentment from a wonky jaw.

From here, the shadow climbs as the last rays of the sinking sun reach higher. A warmer glow. M opens the skylight and cool air drops past his body like fabric. The hill, just visible through the window.

He watches until the peak gently lights like a candle.

Men Like That

Help wanted.
Apply Whithin

Sellotape squeaks from the roll, teeth-torn strips crackle. It snags, plastic and sweet in his mouth. A thumbnail digs it clear and he flicks it with his tongue. It sticks to his lip. M sees his mistake. He spits the shred to one side and scribbles a correction before smoothing the tape down.

The inward-facing picture of the faded postcard glows as he closes the shop door. A sweeping golden beach and the ink of his handwriting bleeding through, hovering, reversed in a half-toned sky.

The cost of this extra wage occurs to him. His usual mental double-entry checks and balances are shrugged aside, for now.

He figures that village money just gets passed around, it never multiplies. The shop has long been part of the churn, and to older customers he is still the *shopkeeper's-boy* shopkeeper. His father's mantra is his own now: answer questions; find solutions; clean up messes; be useful; take pride. Be honest.

He makes himself needed, provides the right tools for a job, offers credit to the disinherited, sees all sides of feuds or squabbles. He solves problem gutters, stained carpets, woodworm; he offers a fix for engines, livestock, leaks. He holds a ledger of the village.

But every day the village tells him that, of course, *men like that* are born liars, untrustworthy, against nature, effeminate, weak. Light in their loafers, shirtlifters, nancies, benders. *Men like that* are a menace. Buggers. Keep children safe, boys away. Abusers. Corruptors. Perverts.

Sooner shoot their sons than father *men like that*, meting out disgrace in everlasting fire. Sinners, sodomites, unnatural and debased. Papers shout of abominations, a disease, a cancer, a terror, a time bomb, a plague, of *men like that* swirling in the cesspit of their own making. *Men like that* are grossly indecent. *Men like that* should be locked up, hung, stuck, castrated. Every day some customer or another tells M, this *man like that*.

Keeping shop hours, he is the ear of the village, the listener. They never register his life at all, upstairs in that one room. For them he lives down here, ready to serve at the counter. His name and his job are connected, like two straight lines that form the corner where he stands. *Jones-shop*.

He flips the sign to OPEN and it taps against the glass as the door-fixed bell diminishes. The hopeful invitation in place. An extra pair of hands, a new pair of hands.

Help wanted, B reads.

The invitation is understood and accepted.
The card is amended—
Vacancy Filled

Sheep

The van is full and low-slung on creaky suspension, lurching between reedy ditches along a winding thread of tarmac. They are out to pick up a paint order, driving across the high plateau of the Common. Stocky wild horses eye them as they pass. Startled lambs dive into bracken guided by ewes.

The journey is easy, both men self-consciously amiable on the road. Radio takes the place of any real conversation. Music, news and quizzes prompt comments, singalongs. A way of navigating things not said yet.

M had picked up B that morning. Conscious of the van rattle as he had turned into the small close, too loud a sound in the morning stillness. He cut the engine. He was early.

A small patch of lawn littered with piled boxes and bin bags in front of the house. A gull-spilled sack of clothes and shoes.

He fidgeted with the controls. Casually.

Nervous, excited, he sensed movement behind the patterned glass. He turned the key and the engine jumped into life. A red cap at the door, a nod, a smile. Keys jangled and the suspension bounced as B pulled himself into the passenger seat, dropping a carrier bag in between them.

B nodded at his dad's house—
S'a mess isn'it?
— his tight voice light, shaped as a smile.

M reciprocated, meeting the familiar dizziness of loss, of grief.

His own father held him close after his mother passed. *Jones & Son*. He grew up quick, play siphoned into the shop that filled his days and busied his sleep. His options narrowed onto the path left by his father's slow exit from the shop. And now it's just him. The *& Son*.

B tuned the radio.

Bloody 'lectric's cut off.

Got to find somewhere new. Now Dad's stuff's cleared, I drop off the council list.

A hiss stuttered through broadcaster voices toward music.

Sunglasses slide to and fro on the dash as they swing along the track on their return. The low sun is shaded by visors stuffed with paperwork. A Magic Tree freshener hangs from the rear-view, sugaring the smell of diesel, sweat and worn leather. The fake-pine scent reminds B of the walk, that first day, the forest.

Windows down, their elbows lean and easy hands stream warm air as the hills open up ahead.

M brings the van to a halt roadside. It judders as the engine drops and the stopped noise lets different sounds into the hush. A skylark rolls, high and pure.

Rest for a bit?

They stretch, relieved, slide the side door of the van and sit. Two cans of cold beer in the heat of the spring sun. Eyes forward, they say nothing, intensely aware of the land ahead of them. B rolls a cigarette and glances up. They face the highest point, *Carn Bugail*.

They recall the awkwardness of that first meeting. The hope and anxiety, like magnets reversing poles, pull close then part. They have lost a lot of time to worry since that new year. In turn they discounted it, the idea of anything happening – that there is anyone like them. Perhaps they misread things, or it's imagined. Maybe they are mistaken. But what if they're not?

M closes his eyes to the sun. He's relaxed more than tired. Lets out a sigh and leans back in the warmth, pushes off his trainers and opens his shirt.

B glances. Hairy chest. A pot. Not fat, but solid.

He looks longer, unobserved, and remembers the book that sat on bedroom shelves by his brothers' bunk. It had been tucked between kids' stuff, passed down the line of siblings, dated and torn and coloured-in and babyish.

This book would fall open where the cover was bent, pages cracked with glue and stitching. It smelled different to the other books. Ink-dense photographs, like oil.

Rich full-page studio film stills between comic strips, grown-ups, spies, guns, cigarettes and flesh.

The book hadn't seemed all that interesting when he was small. Then he couldn't stop looking at it. He saw his brother looking too, at page sixty.

On page sixty a woman rises from the sea in a strappy bikini, holding a large pink shell, the sunlight in her hair, her feet in soft sand.

When his brother wasn't there, he turned the page. On page sixty-three, the hero sits on the edge of a biplane. In trunks. B stared at the mass of chest hair and seawater-slicked tanned skin.

Where the glue perished, the book eventually fell in two. His brother's page ended the first half, but the second half started with the secret agent squinting, smiling.

B knew then he shouldn't talk about it but hadn't figured why.

He rolls the beer can over his forehead to look sideways again, the sun low and bright in his eyes. The metal of the van clicks and ticks. The warm smell of tyres and tobacco. The beer is cool in his mouth and he lets it pool on his tongue before swallowing.

M rests, eyes closed. B reaches over and pats the belly next to him with a smile. First contact.

You'll need to eat less chips now you're employing me, I'm pricey.

M swallows a gassy burp with indignant raised brows, but a smile is returned, one eye open.

They slowly tread out into new territory. M leans and shuffles nearer and they sit again for a long time. Motionless, comfortable silence.

A car comes into view, tracing the contours of the hill opposite.

The mood clouds.

They sit up and shuffle apart. Swiftly they swig and crush cans with a twist. Stand and get back into the van. Amiable again. M stares straight ahead, his hand on the gearstick.

The sheep shouldn't be this far up, he says, as the van shudders into life.

He looks at the carrier bag of B's stuff – barely there. He wouldn't take up *that* much room.

I can make space at the shop you could rent.

He hears himself say it, surprised at his own words.

If you're stuck, like.

Doubt

The man could not tell anyone. That's one of the rules.

B stepped into the cubicle, a warm wooden seat and his school tie, uncomfortable, twisted in a knot.

He started small. He listed his sins in order of bigness. Stammered as he began.
He has sworn.
He has fibbed to his mam.
He has been mean to his sister.

Then he said what he thinks he is.

A silence.

The only person he had ever said it out loud to said nothing.

Sour breath and armpits and stale cigarettes filled the air.

Then a soft voice on the other side of the mesh. Soft and coaxing, but full of damnation and hell. *There's no place with God if he chooses that path. He should try harder. He should be patient, wait for the right girl. Touching himself is a sin.*

His hands moved away from his body quickly, as though they might do something he couldn't control.

Ten Hail Marys and silent prayer.

Punk

B clears the medicine cupboard before leaving. A papery *thuck* as the bag fills – *twice a day before food. One three times daily. External use only. A pea-sized amount.* Sachets and droppers and tsps. Tubes and bottles and boxes and the shock of Dad's full name in print.

He pictures how he would have introduced him to his new boss, his landlord, M. The two men would shake hands, nod. Job done.

He drops the bag into a street bin. Sorry, Dad.

He thinks how pleased Dad would have been about the new job at the shop. He was pleased back when B stopped being a sullen teen, pleased when the scruffy black clothes wore out. Pleased because he had felt a failure when things hadn't worked out at home.

His boy was neither a grafter nor academic, his boy drank more than stolen beers, slugged colourless drink that tasted of aniseed, forgotten in a drinks cupboard, then sobbed and fought, small and weak and angry. The boy who hid from everyone in his drifting family, from him. A boy who found Airfix glue and tried to hyperventilate a high, but burned his nose. B, who stole cigarettes from his mam. *Same as your brothers*.

School was endured until it wasn't. Doodling, distracted, B was a daydreamer. The lure and terror of leaving the village evaporated with every low-grade failure. Lost, disappointed, he tried a swagger, but he was mostly quiet, passed off as moody. He wanted to swear and spit and steal. It was easy to be wayward. Valleys wayward. He didn't understand why everyone was so uptight.

He dressed up to dress down, careful and careless. He lost himself in raw music, noise, guitar riffs and gigs and gangs. He followed the tail end of the comet of energy his sister knew first hand.

The music took him a step away from himself. A misdirection. A wrong target that hid the real reasons he was angry and sad, why he downed syrupy-coloured cheapshit vodka. He couldn't be *the same*.

After years of his dad, *no clue, same as your brothers*. After *get your hair cut* and *wear something smart*. After his dad taking him to a training scheme in a building that smelled of soup and carpet tiles, to sit alongside big men more used to industry at rows of undersize desks to be reskilled, *Writing a CV on a word processor.*

Directionless, he filled his dad's bungalow, feet up.

In the *for-best* room the only books on the shelves were a set of *Encyclopedia Americana*, sold door-to-door, instalment by instalment that came with him from Mam's house. She paid when she could, but the salesman called round too often, so H through to L was missing.

Idly, he looked up forbidden words.

Fuck wasn't listed. *sex. testicles. bum. anus. penis. masturbate.* He looked up *punk*.

Punk: synonym of catamite: a younger man with an older as a (usually passive) homosexual partner. . . If he is small and weak, he may decide to become a 'punk', derogatory, *synonym* of faggot: any male homosexual.

There he was, not the same. The trap closed.

Shop

These early months set the rhythm of being newly together. Their working agreement is informal. B is learning by doing, on the job. All new to him, the shop and its stock are articulated, demonstrated. Shown off.

The roles are definite but unspoken.

M works at the counter. He's meticulous, identifies the right hinge or handle from a description, offers the correct glue for the job, the solvents, the waxes and stains. His voice is low and confident about stonecutting blades, the right nails for slates, ringworm treatment for sheep, getting tics from a collie. It's the village's only hardware shop, an ironmonger, that sells a bit of everything. Browse long enough you always find what you need. Except food. He is not licensed to sell food, only pet supplies that hum with a mealy meaty fierceness, like a fleshy brewery. Ironmongers *& Fancy Goods*. The add-on his own, in a different font. A fancy font.

Patter, advice, the *ting* of the till. Gossip from the two chairs that face the counter by the door, placed there years before, his father's innovation.

Happy away from this chatter, B handles stock, bulky farm deliveries, paint orders. He can signwrite, sharpen knives, occasionally turns his hand to shoe repairs.

There are no *private* or *staff only* signs. The division between front and back is not set, but there is a very clear difference. Shop floor, sales – and the yard.

B tightens the clamps on a board to be primed. He lightly strokes his thumb across the blade of the plane, runs it along the edge of a wooden frame and his body follows with even pressure. He's learning how to use each tool sold in the shop, methodically, on his own.

Under instruction, taught, he always feels stupid, slow.

Even now he shudders at the thought of school, it brings back the smell of sick, of Jeyes Fluid, milk and wet coats on pegs. He liked to draw when he first started. There were big sheets of paper and paints and he wanted to do just that, and nothing else, to copy wrong-looking Disneys, to see his pictures go up on the walls.

He remembered the smell of crayons, of powder paint, of ink flowing from the marker pens. He remembered licking them when no one was looking, tasting colour.

But he trailed behind, made to sit on his own in the library because his spelling was not so good. They tried to get him to tell the time, but when he looked hard all the numbers swapped sides and he couldn't recall which direction the hands moved round. He knew where lunchtime was, when they met at the top to make one line.

Soon, he was sitting on his own most of the day. Teachers called him his brothers' names, one after the other until they remembered his. Filled with everyone else's chatter, his mind drifted and wandered.

He was in the toilet, with his best friend, washing hands, untucked and laughing. Peeing the highest and telling each other secret things. They giggled and made fart noises, soap fired from slippery hands with a *plup*.

The teacher shouted, red faced, and slapped their legs. Made them stand on a table with their shorts down all afternoon because they smiled at her rage. It was not a joke, learning.

He sweeps the clean edge of the plank. The smell of resin and pine is pungent and the perfect curls of wood fall to the floor as the plane runs its course. With a job to do, and time to do it, the learning grows. He is excited by it, by the shop.

A language of admiration builds between the two men for the well-sharpened blade, the balanced hammer. A satisfaction in a square that is true. In the finest needle or the heaviest pick, in his dexterity, possibility and understanding. An extension of his hand, of touch.

Tigr

The old cat wanders from counter to yard, into the warm. She turns her back and stiffly settles. Blinking in the sun, lopsided but comfortable next to B, curious at the new activity. M watches from the shade of the shop.

Tigr, last of a long line of mousers. Sometimes ratters. M remembers the soft rope of bones that flicked, lazy and tolerant of his small hands, remembers how big spines felt under the smooth and resist of tawny fur. Shop cats were the sentinels of his childhood world.

FREE TO GOOD HOMES, read a card in the window each year. Kittens were kept by the towel-warmed cardboard boxful in the outside toilet. Blue sticky eyes, mewling, abandoned to an unsteady crawl and fall. Forgotten in their mothers' on-heat she-cat prowl, her ears turned to their calls, but not her head. At night she hunted every dark corner, rested by day in shop-window yellow sun, draped over stock.

Back then the shop was all still to discover, for the cat and M. They would weave through the boots of rough-faced men, tasting the world in anything dropped to the floor. Bony, rattleskull hands mussed his downy hair from above. Then he was lifted into their world and paraded, shy and not shy.

He remembers the feeling of abundance. His parents had waited so long for him. Others had been expected and never came. They grew older and hope faded. Then, when she first held him, his mother said she had never felt so young. The year he turned nine, the black mountain swallowed the school and the children. That year she said she would never, ever let go. He was her abundance and his father's pride.

The cat scratches her ear. She stays in the yard, the shop. Never upstairs, fleabag.

Never upstairs.

Split level

Over time, B finds other unmarked boundaries – just as there is a backyard separate to the shop, so there is an upstairs and down. There is a shop-kettle, and there are shop-mugs, shop-biscuits – all belong downstairs. Theirs and not theirs.

The division between B and M is less clear above, the partition between them flimsy. B's small room lodged in the corner of a bigger bedsit. One in the other.

He stares at his still-packed bags, unopened all these months. His old life crammed in this small space. Little more than a cupboard filled with a small bed. He sits on the daisy-pattern fabric. Familiar, handed down. Not much that is his own here yet. A few tapes, a clock from home and this childhood quilt, threadbare and worn. A link to his mam, it moved with him to Dad's, and now here.

He wishes he could tell her what he feels. He tried, with a dry mouth he fluttered and hesitated for days, anxious for the right moment. She noticed, imagined he was coming down with something and coddled him. Time off school, aspirin, Lucozade in a sticky bottle. He didn't interrupt her kindness.

He tried so hard to not be one of those names hurled around school. Even thinking it, his face burns with shame.

He hears M moving just the other side of the thin wall, cooking. He blushes a deeper red.

He remembers the advert in the back of a music magazine. *Hypnosis. Heal any illness through the power of the mind.* A cassette tape, from America. Send a cheque or postal order – *guaranteed*.

He saved up for weeks. He lied. Lied to his mam. She wrote a cheque for him, *for a music tape* he told her, pouring coins into her hand.

You, you and your music.

He lay in his bunk, under his quilt, with a drawling voice on headphones. The universe, the hurt we cause, and how we can heal ourselves. At the right moment, as instructed, he pictured his illness surrounded in bright pink and blue lights that wrapped it up and lifted the thing he can't name out of his body.

It felt ridiculous. He felt sick but kept trying, night after night, to fix himself. That voice, again and again until the batteries ran low and it distorted like a drunk into a lurid, exhausting murmur. Nights blurred and days slipped.

It didn't work.

He woke slowly one morning from a dream. In it, the man, the American man on the tape, is behind him, whispering close to the nape of his neck. On the pillow the cassette still spewing itself in spools, a tangled metal-sheen scribble. The covers were wet and his pants stuck to his belly.

The voice stopped. The pink and blue lights went away.

The memory of it leaves a tight feeling in his gut. He stares at the flowered quilt cover, chosen by his mam all those years ago. He gets up and shakes the fabric over the single bed. He can smell frying. He closes the door behind him with a click. A paper stack of price lists slumps across the floor.

Workingmans

Just one, just one. Okay, I'll have another. Fuck, it's my round.

B stands in a group at the bar. His brother at his side.

Easy with people he knows, smoking. Those things he keeps at the back of his mind start to lift in the fug of drinking. His place at the shop, his place in his new home, M. Needing to find out what it is he is going to do and go and do it, whatever the risk. He is biding time, but maybe mistakenly. The people he trusts might understand the truth. He looks up and his brother puts a fresh pint down for him on a bar towel, wet with run-off.

Up y' bum!
His brother's glass drips froth in a stream that *pat pat pats* the floor tiles.

Resolve sinks comfortably into resignation as B lifts the drink to his lips. With each sip, the shop, the world and the worries of the day are diluted, then slip away with the light. It's not so bad.

Streetlamps, ghost-grey concrete until the spark of the bulb shifts night from blue to orange. It's late. He hasn't eaten yet. Crisp packets fill ashtrays.

M, no less drunk, sits at a table in the lounge, not the bar.

Across it two men play dominoes, customers at the shop. Others swap news, red-faced hoarse voices grow louder and lewder. B's mam in the snug with girlfriends, generations side by side. Spouse-rid wives and widows lean forward, hiding below hushed voices to burst up through laughter.

New stories, stories they all tell every week. Reactions, pauses, punchlines prepared in seasons of rehearsal. Laughter on cue. Feet outstretched; arms folded. Content.

B's sister arrives with his older brother. They're all here now, less Dad, a full house. It might be a long night. It used to be a *men-only* bar until her sit-in, dance-in, drink-in. The committee relented and she celebrates, every weekend. His siblings tease him—

Why aren't you with anyone yet, baby brother?

We know you're no looker – but still? The rhythm is comfortable, familiar. Family. Running together now, as they did then.

The four of them. They ran together through summers. B had to step fast to keep up.

The light filters green through leaves. He's low to the ground and bracken arcs a canopy. Hiding until his turn to seek.

They kept out of the way, at home, out from under feet.

They crawled into the crumbling drift bored into the hill, coal-black and glinting. They smashed the windscreens of abandoned cars and raked the glass diamonds.

They found a dead sheep in a stream and visited it daily with sticks, watching it shrink and bloat to grin back at them from ragged wool.

The summers were full of falls and leaps and forfeits. Of scabs picked at the edges and tarmac-grit grazes, dock-leaf salve on stings, breath held underwater. Of running alongside trains and freewheeling bikes down the steep rutted tracks. Summers of dares and whispers of what men do and what women do, and who has seen what.

. . . fortytwo, fortythree, fortyfour, fortyfive.

On his own B hid, high up on bales of hay. A rustle in his ear as an insect looked for a home. He didn't move but was aware of his own small body. His breath. His stomach rumbled hollow, his hand resting in his pants, holding himself like he needed to pee. They couldn't find him and suddenly he felt left behind. Extra. He sank lower and stayed hidden.

. . . seven, fortyeight, fortynine, fifty.

Timing puts them at the trough together and for a moment they are alone. Eyes meet, a pause. Toilet doors link the bar and the lounge at either end. The jukebox bursts a muffled Morse message at the open and close. Eyes front again. A loud lad talks to his mate. Aiming, deeply interested in the tiles, in scraps of scrawled graffiti.

They perform escapology in reverse each time they leave the shop, tucking themselves into the world. Back in the box, chains tight and key safe. They're co-workers. Socialising is dangerous. Not a glance. Nothing familiar, nothing that could be misconstrued.

They don't look at each other as they perform innocuous work-related small talk. A coded hello of delivery times, boxes that need moving and new orders for signwriting. No risk. All the while shoes soak up piss from the floor and the dot-dot-dash of music underscores their mute communication.

A song he knows. A shake and drips splash. *Zip*. B sings as he heads back to the bar.

The night gets messy.

More drinks than should happen on a weeknight.

The shop is silent when B returns. At the foot of the stairs, the sentinel Tigr wants to be fed. Her eyes follow his unsteady tread. He raises a finger to his lips at the creaking step. As he climbs he can hear the snores of M above and catches sight of his own distorted smiling face in the porthole mirror. Stops.

Then his grin widens as he tiptoes on careful feet to pull his weight on the banister, up past M, in this room above the shop.

Spit

Spit and awkwardness. It isn't how B pictured it over the years in his excited mind. The weight of M. Legs and arms tangled hopelessly. He feels pinned. Inflexible. Stabbed.

Taut muscles relax as feverish desire shivers and blooms. A rub of hair and skin and warmth. Another body, a grown body with scars and sinew. Eye contact, a push and rock. He feels his thighs, his guts and toilet. Naughty, dirty, shameful. The mud below. Sodom and hellfire.

The pressure outside matches a new sensation in his belly.

He finds the thing he had fantasised over in shame and sinning, but all that heat and breath and grunting can't be sin. This thing is happening. They are both laughing, smiling. Kissing.

M intense in the rise and fall. A face, even now showing small white flecks in dark stubble. The heat builds in his body and a heartbeat rushes through his head, pulses in his hands and his balls. The skin taste and slight touch of hair and lips lick-suck-tug search.

They lurch and drop over the peak at the same time in a hushed groan and whimper. Tense, the flex and judder, and seaweed smells of semen and spit and blood and food all capsize as they slump and sink sleep-deep.

The first. It's a world only they know. The place they have for each other. A refuge, a hide. No word or deed reaches the ground from this floating platform, on this mattress, this raft, on this ocean adrift in the afternoon sun. This room lightly tethered by stairs.

Dance

By daylight they move around each other in the tight space they share. Unsure of the limits, unsure how to be. Together they are bashful, apart they are lonesome.

The words feel strange to speak. What are they now? No longer just co-workers, they are friends. More than friends. Gradually, then suddenly all at once, they are embarrassed in front of each other. Their bodies surprise them with aches and muscles they haven't noticed before. They know how a day's work smells on the other. They make attempts at taming hair, at smartening up.

They try to talk. M blushes. He falters, his tongue unable to shape the sounds. They open up shop and it's an escape, a pause at least. The discovery they've made between them feels fragile. B looks for reassurance. Both worry that things might change.

Night by night naming things is easier. The box room discarded, unneeded, they live in one space. Close together and hidden in darkness they speak their thoughts, experiences, fears.

And in each day, every look is significant. Everything secret, charged in tension and excitement. They clench in dread of exposure. A lip-biting silence above the shop, even alone. Nervous when someone passes on the street below, as if they can be sniffed out, heard, read. It must be written on them, a target. A *not*.

The world is worn inside out, as though everything is on display. Food and breath, the sap from trees. Warm earth. A scalp against a body. It is intoxicating. Scent is intense, almost visible. It wraps, tugs, makes them aware of the grit and slick of the world, the salt of a lick and the sweat and spill of pleasure.

New-found, everything is their sex. Each day a torture of behaviours resolves when they are together, when beer slakes thirst and privacy eclipses inhibition.

Questions keep their eyes locked and limbs close. Laughing at a boyhood logic of sticky-out bits and sticking-in bits, the joy of plugs and sockets, of things that fit together. Bodies unshown are now seen, raw as peeled apples. A touch that gently seeks every pock, every scar, every patch of hair, tracing the tangled line toward a belly button that joins them to family, to mothers. B re-tells his dad's awkwardness, the *chat* and the *wait for the right girl*.

Only when shame finds them in that room, spread there on the bed, it changes.

Something clumsy and sad makes their movements awkward and broken. They are rougher, functional, aware of themselves. Eye contact is less, but the pleasure equal. Boys being dirty. Boys being filthy. Men who have sex with men. *Men like that.* Tears pool with saliva. They hold each other close. Boys together, clinging.

And then pity fades into the curve of a spine, the weight of muscle, the thrill of the skin between their legs that fires with an electric charge. The lower back that rises to a cleft, soft and furred. Urgency is never far away.

The wrestle of being held tight and close in those days, as the nudge and push of arousal finds a home. They find the places where the outside meets the inside. Fingers stray around feet, to calves, cupping, stroking and exploring.

They sleep, locked together, to wake as one thing.

Gift

On a tray in the jeweller's window, they are not cheap but they are perfect, identical. Bought for each other at carefully spaced different times – different days, different weeks – to inconspicuously mark an anniversary. One year. A Christmas gift from one to the other to the other, a watch, unfussy and engraved with a single initial on the back. An innocent M, an anonymous B.

Set in perfect time, the hands sweep the same curve, the same speed. A red baton glides gracefully around the face.

Under the leather strap M tucks the list and looks at the time. Shopping is never together. They split it, go at different hours. The wire baskets are heavy with a mismatch of ingredients. Groceries move into the small cupboard. They grow used to odd meals.

Later, up the Workingmans, M is crowded with people who once bought a paintbrush, are grateful for credit or the hello and chat. They all have a claim. They all have a share, seasonal cheer. B buys his own pint and crisps and checks his watch against the bar clock. He waits, confident, alone, reading the paper.

No one knows the wrist of one carries the time of the other. A present. One of two.

Hypermarché

Fine blue smoke fills the room. B drags a finger through ketchup to clean the plate. Lazy cooking, shared beans and potch. The air is rich with the smell of frying, and windows steam and run. They slouch back in chairs, full. They talk in low voices, planning for their day off, for the shop, New Year. Excitement for what lies ahead. A walk to the highest point, their lookout, together.

M draws marks on a sheet of paper as he talks, circling and tracing them with his finger as he plots. Bright green eyes and stubbed teeth, keen and ambitious.

New jobs – giant DIY superstore to open this spring, the paper announces. They have seen it being built outside town. Blank high walls of rolled steel, automatic doors, no windows.

They both remembered the first *giant* store to arrive, all the fuss. Back then, old Mr Jones didn't see it as a threat.

We've got everything here, mun? Who wants to drive all that way to buy a box of nails?

Do you remember, years ago, the opening? He recalls the panic-buy of a cot, the smell of new, unboxed plastic.

Actually, are you old enough to remember that monkey?

In front of a low building of special offers and cheapness, the monkey stood and roared. The jaw clicked open and shut. It was only pretend, but big and mechanically *alive*.

Hell, yes. I remember the monkey.

Painted lines like ice cream melting at his feet. Thick and pale yellow. He refused to go closer, to take his turn. He wanted to cry. He didn't. His fear has kept every detail super real. A bin overflowed, flies buzzed and settled on fruity sugar. It was the largest place he had ever seen. He was small. It was big.

Serious, I thought it was looking right at me, I couldn't look back. I was absolutely scared shitless.

As dark as the pithead. The hydraulic hiss and sigh of pistons advertising this new giant way of shopping. Like King Kong picking people up and tipping them down into the dark of its crimson mouth. Burying and resurrecting. Burying and resurrecting. He remembers pushing his face into his mam's coat to hide, breathing the comfort smell of her wardrobe and perfume and cigarettes – but the roar reached in for him. Like when the radio lost signal as trains rumbled past and he was left in a noise that separated him from everything.

I just wanted to go home. I didn't want to see the monkey. I probably wet myself.

B pulls on his boots.

Honest.
I was five—
It picked people up and ate them.

A hairy ape the size of a helter-skelter.

M navigates the dishes in the sink, nails scrape food from the pan. He smiles to himself. Soupy warm water swirls with bits.

Plod

M always gets up first, and the sale starts today. His big idea.

He rolls off the mattress and sits drinking tea. He runs hot, always warm to the touch. B feels his weight rock the floorboards as he tries to tiptoe through the bedsit-storeroom naked.

Every morning M washes standing in a baby bath. Lathers up, rinses down. Warm water steams the cold air.

He scrubs bits and pits, rubs vigorously under his balls and around his bum. B watches his hairy ape from the bed. They chat morning-chatter as soaped plums bounce and flop. Rinsing is with a plastic jug. He foams his chin then shaves his cheeks, his neckline down to his shirt as far back as he can reach. He trims his beard and ear hair. Aftershave and a clean shirt.

It isn't a flat, not really. It's a big storeroom, a mattress, the basics and a makeshift kitchen. And a cupboard with the zedbed once set up for B.

There are two rooms above the shop. Of course there are. There are two men. Living together in a small space. How can there not be two rooms? Like a magician's trunk this fact arrives occasionally in conversation, spun on wheels and shown to have no false sides or wires or tricks. It is solid. It is true.

Nobody comes up here to discover only one bed unmade – in a sea of clothes and paperwork – with two pillows, two unwashed mugs.

M gets ready for the day, unpacking boxes for the things he's promised customers. Samples, scribbled notes and receipt rolls bound tight with elastic bands. All the while aware, and pleased, that B is watching every bounce of his penis, still visible below the last button of his shirt. Peacocking is always exciting. The possibility of contact. The chance of closeness.

Here above the shop is ease. He sits and sews a button back on, trouserless. Here he is himself. There, he is performing. This aftershave is for the wives and grandmothers who watch him as B does now. Part of the show.

The Tell

They try to avoid eye contact if the thought finds them.

The look, then the longer look, as they stack box after box of screws on the correct shelves.

Phillips, one-and-three-quarter number eights. *Four boxes.*
Flatheads, brass. *Two boxes.*
Self-tappers. *Half a box left.*

A glance. Quick enough to be missed in the busy shop, but long enough to communicate. A look that keeps them close and apart in the same moment. A secret. A pause.

The sudden bodily yearning for upstairs feels reckless, the contours beneath clothes giddy. A rolled-up sleeve, an overall, a T-shirt riding up, and the hunger starts.

Then it comes, the chase. And it's right there, between them in the shop, and no one sees. Almost unbearable. The wildness of lust, the ride and fall, pressed tight, forehead to forehead and the pulse and twitch of desire.

They still wonder at it, in awe of mouths and tongues and stubble. One body mapped on the other, over and under a shifting landscape of muscle and hair and the skin of their everyday hurt. But the night-time is theirs, repetition their escape, the thrill of another day navigating toward evening.

The threshold is not difficult to bridge. It is crossed in a look. They have been slipping unnoticed from one realm to another all their lives. They are the escapees. Houdini-like they unthread the knots of awkward questions, sleight-of-hand things they dare not name.

In front of customers, a slip, a wrong-foot raises the stakes. It's both a thrill and a threat.

Recovery is everything. M quips, jokes, bargains for time as he finds his way back to the illusion. They know not to fall into traps.

No pauses,
don't over-elaborate,

don't think about upstairs.
Keep eye contact – just enough,
look away – just enough.
Don't look up.
Don't rush.
Follow the flow of conversation,
think forward.
Anticipate where to dive.
Hold on to words and swim back to the surface.

Balance

M leans in the sunny doorway of the yard, looking back through the shade of the shop. His weight on one foot, he gulps the last of his tea. He folds his arms across his chest, an eye on the door to the street. His empty mug hangs on one finger.

He's halfway through clearing the counter. A tuck-away of stuff with no home. Old paper, chewed into mouse droppings that dot the shelves. A decades-old sweet jar of unbankable cash tipped out. Foreign currency, slot-machine tokens, tooth-dented counterfeit pound coins.

His father had started the jar. They had sat at a small table close together, scratching heads. Tails of paper curling to the floor. Decimalisation had arrived. Coins stacked like gaming chips to convert old money into pence. Pee. One-pound-fifty-pee. Stocklists adjusted, everything doubled. A balance found between a son and a father.

The shop scales still have temporary dots and markers, stickers worn away, reminders pinned to walls there even now, covered up. He remembers conversion tables and calculators causing eye-rolls and delight at new values worn by old coins. Are they still in currency, are they being fiddled?

Everything was two entries. Old money. New money. One a bewildering equivalent of another.

His father overcharged and undercharged, mixed up prices, accounts didn't tally. His grasp of it all was weak, so recently left alone without his wife. This change, after all the changes he endured, was too much. He sighed about old dogs and tricks and how he'll leave this to his son.

Brimstone

B rolls paint from his fingers, watching it dry. The smell of undercoat oily on his tongue under sugared tea. Two butterflies. Brimstones – sulphur-yellow – land on purple flower spikes. He sits and watches.

M cuts the gnarled buddleia away every year, but it is determined. Its hold pushes deeper between the bricks and reaches, grip-tight, into the mortar of the shop. It blooms each season from the wound.

Lifting, the insects circle each other, spin and bounce a vortex, dangerous and close. A single engine firing and rolling and gliding and fluttering. One thing, a shared two-beat rhythm. A tide, the moons. The lift of spring air on beating wings.

The fight, the spiral, rises to higher and higher levels then drops close past him. It is magnetic, intoxicating. Each concerned with nothing but the other, obscuring the view, filling the gaze of all four eyes completely.

B's two eyes follow the tumbling blur and he sees the pale yellow bedspread folded over the shoulders of his dad in the last days. He wonders about getting old, about M getting old ahead of him. He imagines them both cocooned in pastel blankets, wondering at each other and the happy thing they have made here.

The butterflies settle momentarily on the doorframe. He feels a wave of love and panic. If one of them was to be ill—

Wings open and close in a flashed bright message to launch again.

Virus

They make themselves read it together. They had seen it a year or so before. Sent to every household, an unmarked envelope dropped through doors. Blank. As if a machine had antiseptically folded it in three, then stuffed and sealed the envelope, without spit, without touch. Unfolded, it felt uncomfortably medical. Like something to be pinned up at the doctor's waiting room.

This one is under the counter of the shop. The leaflet has a tea-ring stain, joining the A, the I and the D. *The virus can be passed from man to man—*

A black marble slab, the ad. A tombstone. The Iceberg. *So far it's been confined to small groups—*

Chiselled stone. It's all so cold. Drugs and needles and condoms and advice. Both men feel ignorant. Naïve. Everything feels dangerous.

Is what they do a risk? – *defence against the disease depends on all of us taking responsibility for our own actions. Don't Die of Ignorance.*

They are scared. The fear is a low rumble, a tremor. They feel like every headline they see is about them. *Full blown. A plague.* Their plague.

The village is reading about them.

They must already have it. Or they'll get it. Or it's their own fault. They deserve it. What if they fall apart? What if this is too much or too little to feel and people notice?

Fear brings them closer. Hands rest longer on parts of the body that might once have blushed or recoiled. Advancing and retreating, the anxiety subsides. Their life moves away from furtiveness, but remains a secret, remains theirs. They spend longer connected, longer together above the shop.

The Third Stair

The third stair up from the shop floor is rotten. Cracked and woodworm dusty. It gives underfoot, a squeal and snap as the split worsens.

The plastic ribbons screen them from the shop, a curved security mirror halfway up. It shrinks the two worlds into one dome, each visible from the other. A flyblown separation of their work and home.

They are steep, the stairs. At the top, four steps narrow into wedges and half-turn. Tucked into the crook of each are small piles of paper, tools, biros, boxes. Stuff to go up, stuff to come down, stuff doing neither.

B finds love in the strength of his friend, held high in the crog loft of the shop. What is love if it isn't the bed on a sea of manilla bills and payments, if it isn't the mugs of tea carefully delivered, and the makeshift den they have made?

What is love if it isn't the shop and its systems and classifications, its order and its chaos, its pauses and its patterns? Above it they are true, held up by the staircase that is the threshold of their world.

They share a rhythm, up and down. Right foot, then left, a grip on the bannister and a stretch to avoid the third step. Like badly timed Foley on an old film, strange feet miss the beat.

An early warning.

Pierce

B stays busy, head down. Boys he knew at school, no longer boys, shoplift. M catches his eye, a twitch toward them. Lighter fuel and glue and spray paint. They eye him through shelves. They know him. *Punk.*

B touches the lobe of his ear and remembers the drawing pin. Blu Tack. An ice cube and a plaster. The boy who compass-stabbed his own biro-ink tattoo in front of the class did it for him.

Which ear? This one. *Wrong.* You bent or what?

As sudden as a sting. Laughter.

He recoils at the memory, all eyes on him. He borrowed the look on everyone else's face, loaned their disgust at the idea.

He hated his year at that school. A Catholic brick hut, but his mam was pleased one of her children had gone.

Long lapsed, she had mouthed prayers to the patron saint of lost causes to get him in. He felt the separation, pushed from his brothers and sister. She made sure to tell the priest about her prayers to St Thomas Aquinas for learning and bought a St Christopher medal for his journey.

But he was on his own there.

He remembers sitting still. Sitting still, firmly held down, letting the boy do it. Sitting still, laughing along like the others. The pain was sharp. He pretended it was nothing. He bled a lot, used his black rugby shorts to stem the flow on the bus home.

That's where he learned. Learned all the things he needed to hide. If he got the wrong ear pierced, if he touched a boy's hair, if he had fingernails, if he looked at his fingernails the wrong way, if he didn't smoke, or didn't smoke a certain way, if he threw funny, ran funny, caught funny, if he drew, if he sang, if he said a word differently, dressed differently, wore a watch on the wrong wrist. If he cried.

Better to not get an ear pierced, to stay away from people, chew his nails, smoke like his dad, practise throwing and catching, dress like the others, do nothing exceptional, speak like the others, never wear a watch on either wrist. Survive. Play along.

He watched how the others were and he made his body move the same, he blended in. He felt like he was pilot of something he didn't know how to steer. He didn't understand everything that was going on. He monitored himself all the time. He was exhausted, spoke even less. Whenever he heard himself out loud he felt like he was going to slip, so his accent mimicked their accent and slowly his voice disappeared. He was hidden and safe. He failed, fell further behind. He let conversation peter out until he was completely alone.

His ear burned red for days until his sister sorted it out. She tried a small silver stud, but it started to smell funny so she took it out. There is still an off-centre dent, a scar where tattoo boy's aim was careless.

Flush

M stays busy, head lowered.

A wedding ring creases her podgy finger as she folds out the newspaper and stabs at the headline. Three customers huddle and nod in disgust. *Outrage!* the article runs. A moustached face is kissing Eros and other men-men women-women clinch and cheer.

M eyes the upside-down page, embarrassed by the kissing, by the defiance. Immediately he's ashamed of his own shame. Pride so far from here, from him.

Rain trickles from bright umbrellas to puddle on the floor. B is upstairs, hidden in their bed. The women bristle, indignant at the tabloid.

He feels adrenaline rise and checks himself. He wears his smiling, deadpan shop-face and looks at the three unkind customers. The same customers who, years before during the strike, came to him for credit with watery eyes at a time when stock sat unsold on shelves week after week. When dust rings marked occasional sales and the yellow blinds kept labels from fading, hiding him inside.

It had lasted months, nobody could pay for things. Everything was on tick. Desperation looked everywhere in hunger and purposelessness and the village came to him, relied on him.

The dispute had solidified into stasis. Benefits and support and solidarity. A stand-off. Slow days in relentless torpor, he waited alone at the counter where credit notes stacked higher than receipts.

With trade so slack he thought he would have to close for good. Most days he would leave a note on the door and wander the village. Help out where he could.

Back in 5.

Built into the wall at the edge of the village was a urinal. It's still there. A civic leftover of upstanding mine owners' efforts at enlightenment through toil. It is a walk-through pisser. Out of place, a continental utilitarian screen and stall.

The floor grits sharp at his step. Sand on tiles. Cool air, like the mouth of a cave, but a stagnant ammonia sting. Flush splash pools in the centre of the floor. A steady *drop drop drop* of water into water. Glass bricks filter leafy gloom. Pipes furred with limescale bloom, copper green on glazed bricks. Spidery marker-pen scrawls and Tipp-Ex band names.

He recalls *that* day.

It is still so vivid. The butterfly gently turning, web-caught old and dry, the flaked, broken colour of a tortoiseshell. Unhurried, he had relieved himself, a satisfying steady stream steamed. Shouts of children playing far away rang from the tiles like a distant radio. It was *that* day when he noticed a brown envelope tucked at the back of the cistern. Pushed in, trying to be hidden.

The familiar blue-back pattern of playing cards, but not a full deck.

He expected the J, K, Q, Ace. Numbers and hearts and spades and diamonds and clubs.

Even now he can still feel the bodily lurch he felt then, like vertigo, as he turned them over.

Each card was a naked man. Men with crooked teeth and promise, clutching and exaggerating, bent over to look back at him. The Joker, the seven, the Queen. These were not coyly posed beefcakes. These were seedier, colours too garish, an eagerness too vulgar.

He was shaking, breathless. He sat down in the stall, still and silent. Was this a trick?

On the back of the door a hastily drawn cock and balls spurted endlessly.

This was him. A mix of arousal and guilt as he shuffled hand after hand of debased bodies. This was why he thought he was better alone for so long. He hid the pack deep in his pocket. Holding his breath. Against the stench. Against fear.

He had faced it for the first time, long before he met B.

Liar, Liar

A ball of shiny wrapping paper bounces off the bin, torn in frustration.

Cheap Xmas shit—

B cuts a new piece from the roll. Cassettes are easy for his sister, boxes are neat for his brothers, but the thin slippery wrap rips and wrinkles rolled around the scarf for his mam.

Cross-legged on the floor they lean over the small heap of presents. M tucks edges, folds fat-robin gift tags. Sticks on shiny rosettes.

Sometimes it's hard to know when their story starts. The story they tell. It's not dishonest, but it is set, the beginning, sometime in the past. It's more than acting, when they are not alone, even with family. Especially with family.

They know where the edges of the stage drop and always find their mark. They shift behaviour, the first step in fitting in; mimicking, blending, passing; things never said. They know the characters who sit where they sit, know the script.

B is the apprentice.
M is the shopkeeper.

Respect and deference, they play their parts day in, day out. In public they stay near enough for prompts but far enough apart. The right distance apart.

There they are in overalls and on tea breaks at the warehouse and wholesaler's, gaffer and boy. A man mopping the floor sways along snaking wet lines, looks up at them standing together. M steps away from B, who reads his cue, his instruction, and busies himself with boxes.

Cracking the whip is he? Lazy bugger. You do all the work and the boss stands there chatting—

In time the version they tell shapes in their minds. Weaves between the facts, fills the gaps and becomes true.

The truth lies parallel, it threads far beyond their lives above the shop. For each of them it snags on every encounter, every deflection, every omission since childhood. Always lying. Exposed, they would be shamed. Shamed in the town that knows their fathers and their mothers, their brothers and sisters and their pets, and all the stories, lies and missteps they have ever taken as children, as boys, as men. It would mean leaving.

Christmas week apart feels a fair price.

Part

Finish them up, go on—

A spud drops onto his plate from Mam's fork. B's brother mops gravy at the pan with a fistful of juicy bread. *Mammy's boy* he mouths, wiping his chin with the back of his arm.

So, when we coming round then? Give Mam a break from cooking the turkey—

Seriously, coming to mine isn't an option – we have to share a kitchen, a toilet, all of it, anyway he's funny about keys to the shop.

M walks away from the village. He walks away from the old year toward the highest point, toward their rock. The day is short and the sky heavy. Purple clouds pile in dim yellow half-light.

He is alone, undisturbed. He wishes they could be together this year, imagines B's family, their shared codes and in-jokes. He smiles, for them.

Tied to the shop, hidden upstairs, he sometimes thinks of the two of them out in the world. A pair. A happy couple whose first date was a picnic in the clawing cold, warmed by eagerness.

Ha! date—

As he climbs, cold rain pats his head. He opens his palm. It's not rain but gritty dust-filled sleet. He heads for shelter in one of the derelict warehouses.

Sleet becomes hail, a sharper sound, it bounces where it hits. He climbs up crumbling breeze-block steps. Under cover, he waits in a loading bay, like a deserted platform at a railway station. The shop and all its pressures and busy-nesses are paused for a few days, but the quiet room above is no comfort when it's empty.

Pelted foliage quivers.

B, so far away, so impossible and near.

White bullets of ice gather in ruts.

This building is long abandoned, a large door leans and rots on its rollers. Silvered light filters in through dark, moss-covered skylights. His breath clouds damp cold air. Hail drums on the rusted metal roof, sound grows.

Water finds its way in with a regular tick. He sits patiently, waiting for the deluge to stop.

On a panelled wall, a faded calendar moulders over June. A surly, hairy farmer forces a smile, sat on a pristine blue tractor. An ear-of-barley logo is peeling away from reeded glass. This was once a supplier of tools and feed. It must be twenty years since he and his father were here. His father's friends were his customers – are his friends. He feels like he was too long alone, before B.

He thinks about sex. He's thought about sex a lot recently. Contact with a body not his own. The excitement of B and the smell and taste and sheer bloody joy of it, laughing, grunting toward the deep, content sleep – tangled and poured into one bed-held mess. He stops himself. He feels the familiar twitch for B.

There's something else. A worry. He is lonely stuck between B and his daughter. His bloodline. She could inherit the shop someday, if she wants it. B could be a partner, an equal. He wants to tell her, the thing he can't name or understand fully, but he just can't say it. He wakes himself from dreams in time to stop speaking the words out loud. Anxious. Embarrassed.

He catches his breath, feels himself a thing among things. The office drawers are spilling index cards, chewed, mildewed. Desks and rusting chairs are still paired. Paperclips and cracked rubber bands scatter and rot. He stares, absent.

If his daughter looks, she might find it in his face. The ghost of a lie.

He opens a filing cabinet idly and slides it shut again. *Shhfftd-clnk*. Satisfyingly loud, even in the downpour. He stands, does it again, harder, a slam. Again, this time he kicks it shut. He hammers. He shouts and bellows all the words he can't speak, the dirtier the louder, chest wide open and lungs full of buried passions and rage.

And then he stops, breathless.

Not even an echo.

He moves for the door, determined. The climb is steep and ice stings his ears. He has to get there and shout, for them both.

He strides. Breath puffs ahead of him and the sky softens. A milder front behind the cold, the hail eases into snow. No creature stirs.

As the ground silently covers he thinks of birds above, feathers puffed, of voles and mice in earthy hollows and the seeds waiting to throw out radicals in the spring. He thinks of B in the nest of their bed.

Crew cut

Fingers gently fold the top of an ear and cupped sounds change. A soft palm rests on his warm scalp. His velvet hair, its direction, its nap, clockwise from the crown. A helix around his whole body from his eyebrows to his toes.

An amber glow from a blanket of white.

Low winter sun at the window and their second anniversary passes.

The buzz of the clipper wavers as it finds stray hairs that curl and escape.

They swap places. Thick fine hair cuts like wheatstalk. His head resists the gentle push of the blades as the combs shimmer. The power cord is cool as it snakes over his leg. Held still. Bare shoulders and muscle under skin.

Cut hair and bristles drop to the floor with the hush of snow.

Giveaway

B sings along at the back of the shop, louder than the radio. Stacking paint tins, noisy, oblivious. As he swings from crate to shelves he hitches up his jeans and looks across to the counter, nodding a beat.

Guilt rises through M as he leans into the phone. Outside, the spring sunshine clouds over. He knows her voice but her accent sounds put on, performed. She's in company, excited and breathless, asks – needs – his permission.

Your big day – yes, if that is what you want.

He will give her away.

She is so young, sixteen, a girl. She covers the receiver, her muffled voice relays news to whoever she is with. She forgets he's there. M falls silent, doesn't know whether to break the connection. She hangs up first. A monotone pulse hums. A fresh wind whistles through the door sweeping litter ahead of it, the sun-slow-blink from cloud cover lights up the window display. He was so young, a boy. He was her age when he became a dad.

He thinks of her tiny hand in his, her slow step by step up the hill. A tread in double time matched in his laboured pace. Her walk tipped, leaned and tripped in new-found gravity. Fast, then slow. Unpredictable.

She stooped to look at weeds, her new discovery. Small fingers gripped and ripped stems for a bright yellow flower posy. Stop. She offered it to him freely, as freely as she forgot it. Back down the hill, her eyes fell on a silver chewing-gum wrapper and he pushed the flowers into his shirt pocket as he accepted the gift of silver. A growing collection of totems, given in earnest, scattered on windowsills. He still has them.

Two Today!

He remembers the party. A soft spring breeze like today, early March.

Terrible Twos!
Toddler Terrible Temper Tantrum Twos.

Her family, crowded in too small a space. She performed, shy but delighted at her audience. Balloons squeaked and puckered.

He sat her down and the landscape of the table filled her horizon. She pointed at a foil dome with cocktail-stick antennae. At the plastic jug of squash. She looked at him like she does. *Da*, then noticed her own hands and grasped at the chair, reaching them out, feeling the world around her. And she pointed again. He offered her a piece of pineapple. Fingers pushed the juicy fibres apart and moved them toward her mouth. *My da. Dadad.* The sound from her was small as she tested it.

A low room with a step down to the kitchen. A milk-jelly rabbit sat on an oval plate, pink and blind in a mashed-up lawn of green gloop. Beer cans and bottles and ashtrays.

Down again to the yard of neighbours, gossip and laughter. He stood in the yard, smoking and separate. He nodded at the man who stood where he couldn't. The stepfather. *Dad da da*, he heard through the window, and waved to her. Her words were few, this shouted word described everything. Described both of them. Legitimacy. He is genuine. He is still true in this one thing.

Everyone moved back inside as the light clicked off. Hush, their inbreath—

Penblw-app-irthday-i-ti.

Languages bumped and slipped over the same tune.

He stepped aside, making way for the crowded glow of two small candles. The room was stuffy, hot with over-dressed bodies and waxy polish. Pushy older children squeezed past in the camera-moment jostle. He moved further back into the doorway, his view over the tops of heads, all looking away. Cool air sat and waited for him. The hall smelled of coats.

Best for everyone, they had agreed, she would live there.

He slipped out, without goodbyes, and walked back to the shop. He noticed every dandelion that held fast. Yellow between paving and bloom-bright in the gloom.

He can't remember how things happened as they did, nor can he understand exactly why. She found him, reached out and made the move. He didn't step back. Or forward. It was all new and he was a coward.

I'm late, she said and looked straight at him.

He didn't understand.

Months before, in the empty shop, they had kissed. He was shy, hesitant. He wrapped his arms around her and they pulled tight. Urgency moved her hands over his back. They breathed differently. He was lightheaded, embarrassed, adrenaline peaked in excitement and fear. The shop felt tipped, dropped, smashed. Weightless, his heart flipped his body over and over. It happened quickly. It happened just once.

She was kind afterward. They lay still. Her slender fingers trailed places only his own hands had known. His hands copied hers, but they moved too quickly or fidgeted, clumsy on her smooth cool skin. He thought of his father and cried to himself – of his mother, the shop – a wave of sadness.

Late?

She said she was sure.

She didn't want to be with him, she had already met someone else. The surprise of relief, of realisation. A weight lifted, as though he felt the ground beneath him finally, after long falling. It could still call him Dad, if he wanted – the baby.

The word landed gently like a bird.

Baby arrived. He cried, she cried louder. He would do everything he could. She would have a good start, even if it was without him.

He held her and a glow fired his body, his racing heart. He would learn her world.

A safety pin, his clumsy fingers, and her wide unfocused blue eyes. The mess and the delight. The smell of sour milk, yeast sweet and baby powder. Black tarry poo everywhere. He washed his arm, thought of a seabird in a sink with wings stretched out under a hose, helpless and scared.

And he was scared. Pacing, jiggling, coaxing, pleading. This person in his two hands would one day hold things in her hands. Small fingers curled to grip his thumb. A giant, ridiculous, calloused lump.

There was a nest in the yard of the shop, tucked beneath the ivy. They discovered it together. A grass cup of rust-speckled eggs.

He looked at her and the joy he felt was also heavy and sad and lost. He wanted more than anything to be her dad, even if she grew up knowing a different one. He wanted to be a good dad.

Only he calls her *Wren*.

Cell

An RSVP, an impossible plus-one. B feels thrown to the edges, cast out. The invitation left an emptiness in him, unwhole and separate.

He knows it's unreasonable to be sullen. He avoids eye contact for just long enough, returns it late. A mood settles. Illogical and sad.

They both notice it. The room is sharp with frustration and feels too small. Elbows catch on furniture, they get in each other's way. The bed, cramped; small talk too loud. They stare toward the open stairs, gaze up at the skylight.

A plane cuts the sky, a white trail drawn across the square opening to the world. Life beyond is both comfort and irritation. Their eyes don't connect. They pace. It is too hot. Too cool. Too bright.

Agitation has been with them for days and they can't shake it. First one, then the other is at fault. Blame hangs in the corners of the room. A dim light bulb at its centre.

In the silence, every sound is amplified. Food-loud chew and crunch. A page-turn rustle.

Hands fidget-twist at collars.

A foot taps a chair leg.

By night they lie among order forms, receipts and stock and hold themselves tight. Unclose. They sense a rare sadness.

Hiccups, unabating. An elastic band snaps and twangs. Radio drift, off-station.

Restless, weary. Sleep arrives and breath lifts their separate worries to the skylight and the evening, to move away on the rising current of air. They are together in this box. A box held up by the stringers and risers of the worm-eaten stairs.

Moon

In sleep the distance they feel lessens. Intimate and strange the thing between them – solid and fragile and curious. B rests, heavy limbed. His face open, unlined, on M's shoulder, tasting air, swallowing a sigh. His mouth closes and opens.

Staring at the white eye of the moon, M thinks of his mother.

What shall it be? she'd said.
Pancakes? They're a bit like moons—
Sort of.

The hiss of static and those first steps on its surface.

He remembers his awe, his sadness, sitting where she should have sat. He remembers how he used to settle with her, snug. The springs' sag, the armrests worn under her hands. That night passed, heavy in the dark. Instead, his light frame rested against his father, not her, as they sank together.

On a small TV, boots slowly lifted to settle in another gravity.

He couldn't understand the world with his mother suddenly missing. They three had planned to watch it together. The excitement was infectious. Anticipation grew, shared. His father was smiling, excited. She was going to cook pancakes; he would be allowed to stay up.

The bright screen flickered on his father's face. Tears gathered, but didn't fall, his mouth held at a point of swallowing, high and tense. B sensed his father's gaze. The smallest movement transmitted.

He had felt small. His father had felt somehow less – loss had cut his strings and he sat back in his chair clinging to the blanket of his son. Against his boy's cheek, a warmth, a breath in and out. His head rose on the high wheeze and fell toward the deep comfort of his father's belly gurgle. Far away.

He saw the surface of the moon, a white light torn across the picture. A beep. A footprint. On-screen darkness was unending, infinite. Dust moved and he watched it rise but not settle.

In the village beyond the window, the dawn chorus. Birdsong, underscored by the broadcast drone, the low murmur of excited experts. Their words dragged like an anchor through sand. Glowing figures ghosted. A crackle.

They numbly watched. The boy and the man.

M felt his role in the family shift as the sky grew light. After that summer he hadn't gone back to school. He attended to his father, heard him at night. A low crooning sigh like an animal lost from the herd, a lone bird without the turn and tilt of a flock.

A determination to keep his son safe kept his own mind floating in space, halfway across worlds.

Stuck

The heat grows, day after day. White sun casts hard shadows and curls leaves a darker green with no rain. Hot squalls of dust and sand lift and drop. Pallid feet raise the smell of un-socked sandals, too long in storage. Coconut sweat-sweet tacky sunscreen and calamine.

Bright light glimmers on days that slump like mud by night, when sleep is dragged out of reach by hot air. Muggy dreams suffocate movement and propped-open windows only let in heaviness.

Snores and mumbles drift into streets, radio and television soundtracks ride warm currents of wet air along with the clash of dishes and the weary tick of clocks and the sounds of sex. Sounds that once soaked and sank into wallpaper now spill out, uncomfortable rhythms in grunts of effort meet the wail and clatter of stray cats bristle-stiff in heat.

The forecast is stuck.

Days sit still and time is viscous, sticky. Chewing gum strings from hot pavements. Tarmac oozes black and shiny. Bitumen blisters.

Paid work is fragile, rare. Divisions still run deep; picket-angry graffiti still visible, disloyal homes shunned. Pockets are empty, borrowing and mending and patching. Everything feels temporary. Desperate.

Sleeplessness breeds delirium. The high horizon narrower, the valley, smaller. Dust lines contour lost streams. There are hill fires – too often. Boys bring a dead adder down into the village, a trophy on a charred stick.

Shit

It's the longest day of the year. A carnival to release everyone from torpor, and the mood lifts.

M stands in the doorway of the shop and watches the parade roll past. B is across the street, waving and smiling and sunglassed.

There, not-there. Glimpsed between makeshift floats of farm machinery and trucks with poster-paint signs. Three fluoro-green radioactive sheep wave from a pick-up. Proud, M sees B's mam, tucked under homemade woolly bathing-cap ears, lean to kiss her boy. Face-greasy pale green smudges his cheek.

Baa baa bye love, trundle on, she's gone.

Unlikely men squeeze into bastard cushion-cover-tea-towel-old-frock costumes. Robots *boogieboogie* through cardboard masks at Hoover-part ghostbusters. The committee hawks raffle tickets and homebrew; fundraisers in bedsheet-togas shake buckets. Deely boppers on bees in stuffed laddered tights and cereal-packet wings. Crêpe-paper dye runs on sweaty children. Thirsty-hot tinfoil armour.

Shade offers no respite.

Clear white sun burns through a sky as blue as a gas flame.

And then the dark. Raucous boozy shrieks in bonfire light through cigarette smoke clouds.

Costumes spill out.
Fights spill out.

Gropes and falls and fingers and wet mouths hold on to Saturday night until it gives way to a grey dawn.

With sunlight, colour returns. Dew-soaked feathers and shrill stains pock the flattened grass. Mid-morning, the quiet heat is here still, unrelenting in empty streets. Sunday church bells hammer and stomachs churn and gas. Burnt pink faces stagger home, heads bowed. Gossip seeps. Wasps short-circuit sugary rattles from paper cups. The day reheats the night and the clean-up waits for the working week.

At the top of the stairs above the shop they speak in lists, not sentences. They leave themselves behind in the mirror as they begin again. Tasks in order, all that needs to happen, whatever the temperature.

The buzz of flies as the door of the shop opens.

A sickly-sweet smell.

A human shit.

A breath is swallowed. In the shop display a lone fan oscillates, tickling the air with looped yellow ribbon. Freshness, held behind glass, ripples paper tags.

They sluice the step into the road and along the gutter to the drain. The iridescent flies follow the roll of water in short arcs of irritation as the soap scum tides and the steam rises. M takes the yard brush and cleans the pavement apron in front of the shop. The fetid air lingers in their nostrils as they flip the sign to OPEN and return to their delayed list.

They are unprepared when it happens again a few days later.

They speak little. B keeps his head lowered as the water slaps and splashes to repeat the doorstep clean-up.

Customers make them uneasy. They glance carefully at each other, add up all the possibilities, all the risks. They both feel vulnerable.

The next morning, and the next – the same scenario. The same stink. The same smell that clings. It now feels deliberate. A warning or a message.

The situation makes them mute. Conversations tangle, knot and fray. Each has a mind on a past where this was what they'd feared. Are they known? They rise earlier and earlier, the whites of their eyes red. They become more distant but united in worry, stay further apart in the shop. Talk less. They put more space where they had grown ease, calculate interactions. The performance is even more exhausting.

A cloud arrives.

Rain pulls at the bone-dry earth.

A cold front cuts the long summer and torment stops with the torrent. The rain is heavy, streaking the window with dust. Wet light flutters to the sill. B shivers. The leaves wash from the trees and everywhere is slippery, it hits stone and splashes, seeping and bubbling deep into parched soil. A stream runs the road and the river swells toward the sea.

They rationalise it. A dog? A drunk maybe? A coincidence. Perhaps all dead autumns arrive the same, and this one ran no different. Maybe they had found worry where there was none. They breathe. Their pavement is brighter with scrubbing, conspicuous – a light scar of nerve endings.

Skylight

I just don't want us to fall out, is all.

A square of sky floats deep blue, cut out of the dark room.
They have been awake since the early hours. Side by side.
Clouds move softly, touched with orange streetlights.

Did you stack those boxes by the door? You'll need to get those out, first thing.

Checked an' laid out ready, you just got to sign the chit before I go.

You know what I mean though, right?
We cannot say a word. You know we can't or this stops working.
I know, I know.
It was years, living up here with no one.
We can at least walk down the club side by side, I mean, it's not like I wan' to hold your hand.

Did you Z the till last night?
No, you did. You did – picture you doing it.

The patch of blue is lighter and the first rays of sun sharpen the edges of the window. Gulls, inland, drawn by the plough and landfill, circle high above them. They watch from their pillows, motionless. They stare skyward. The birds' keening reaches them, disconnected, distant.

They come back to themselves.

She likes you. Mam, I mean.
As your employer yes, not as someone who, not. . . you know. . .
Fiddles her son?
Ow. All right – anyway it's two-way, sunshine.
That makes it sound—
Exactly though, it is isn't it?
I've heard it all. Bent, ponce, poof. Whatever. I wish I'd the guts – I couldn't back then. Now I'm too *known* – there's other things, the shop, the – there's Wren—
– always other bloody things.
There's you.

Us.

A narrow column of smoke from the roofline. A car – windows down, radio loud – passes then leaves them silent in a mixture of hunger and loneliness. The conversation has stopped and M gets the sense he has stopped it.

A golden diamond of sun on the wall as the sky clears and the pale moon is abandoned to the daylight. An early train slowly gets louder, idling into the station. A distant whistle. They stare at the ceiling feeling nothing for a moment but the lightness of feeling nothing.

There is something paused, something undisturbed between them, held for a moment. The smallest sign. Both relax. Closer, content. Then, at the same time, they move.

Scratching and stretching, their bodies flash through the sunlight, B picks up work clothes from the night before, animated. Stepping into pants, unballing socks with his toes. For him, it's a day out front. He's unused to being at the counter.

Clothes hangers swing and chime as M slips into iron-creased trousers. He pulls a shirt front together. Buttons squeak through pristine cotton.

I put undercoat, primer and brushes on the side to go to your mam. You can take it today if you're going. It's on tick.

M breathes in, shrugs and flattens the suit, too tight over his chest. A confetti carton, too big, distorts his pocket. Stubble rasps the collar. B watches him adjust a tie knot, hiding an unbutton.

I don't feel like I'm up to today.

His lapel droops with a heavy tinfoil-pinched carnation sent by Wren.

What then? What we goin' do? What are you goin' do? Don't get me wrong, all *this* I'm good with. This keeps me going –
you keep me going.
It's jus' this place. Us tucked away up here, all the time. We could go somewhere, do somethin'? Together, for us.

M feels cornered, like his back is against a wall. He feels suddenly irritated by the day ahead without B. He moves his body imperceptibly and they both shuffle apart. The mess around the bed suddenly jars. The sun is growing in the room. White light. Hot and sharp.

Sorry.
For what?
You know. Sorry. For this.

Stumble

Drunk and groggy, B wakes to a voice telling him this is the last stop.
Gotta get off mate—

His forehead leans on a cold window. No more trains. It's a seven-mile walk home to the shop and the air is clear. It's dry but cool. He kicks at rubbish, head down. The sharp click of heels comes and goes nearby.

At the viaduct a girl catches up with him.

She is nice, and as slurry-drunk as he is. Walking the same way, unsteady. She leans and they laugh and weave and he forgets for a moment. In drink, time stretches out, the conversation meanders, fluid and fun. They share smokes. Connections are found, she knows his brother. The stranger gets closer.

Here? Why not, come on. She pulls at his belt and leans on him.

He straightens, he's scared. She wants to have sex. He doesn't. He can't. He feels drunk again, he thinks he's going to be sick. They are at the edge of the houses and he walks ahead. He wants to find M. His throat closes and heat rises in his chest. He can't swallow. She screams after him.

What's the matter with me? You gay or what?

A light comes on behind red curtains. He walks faster, staggering into the road. It feels loud. He feels it echo off the streets. Off the hills.

A striplight flickers into life and a silhouette is framed.

You fucking poof.

He stumbles through the shop door, tripping, and slams the bolt. Head bowed as M rushes down the stairs, still in his wedding suit. They stand a long time in the dark, held tight. A sway. A face buried in the warmth of the other.

B&B

Sand from the beach grits on the lino underfoot.

Room 4, behind me on the left, and *Room 11* on the second floor, she says.

Looking at M, she takes two sets of keys from the board.

Sorry, the family twin's taken. Takes after you doesn't he?

Large wooden key fobs clatter on Formica and seagulls laugh.

So, what time do you both want breakfast?

Behind smiles they flush. They allow the assumption to settle before heading to *Room 11*. Tense, they lie together. A lie on a lie on a lie.

Ribs

Dry heat and the salt tang of sweat.

Neighbourly help offered, and taken, on their Sunday, the only day they have, *the lads from the shop*. A repair, a fix of a hay-loft roof. A sort-of barn-raising.

Dust pales pale skin and steals moisture from tongues. Eyes squint muddy, gritty – pink. Fingers bedded in dirt, stripped by lime and shovels and buckets and a hair-tangled static snap of cobwebs, still pearled with flies.

A crab apple tree has its feet in a cool spring and they join it.

They sag together. The dark earth is littered with a June-drop of small pale fruit. In turns, they *bullop* apples into the water. The orbs roll and bubble along the stream, a bright green glow on moss-rusted stone – slipping in the current, flowing over the water-combed edges to fall to the pool below.

Gangly flies cloud in a rise and fall of dodges and collisions. An afternoon ahead, tired and slow and quiet after an early rise.

bullop

Come on.

B spits dusty spit. Splashing, he tugs off his grey vest, unzips, hop-step-hop one leg, hop, the other – jeans flung. He runs down to the fall; pants drop on a pasty moon.

Come on!

He slips into the water low and soundless. All otter. The cold grips lungs tight until shoulders slide in rippling beats across the deep.

A mist thrown out, refracting light in a halo of colour. He looks up at gods rock. god not God. *Y godwr* – the rising, the spring that starts the river that shapes the valley.

A line of clear liquid rises in each ear and he floats and turns, a pale star in the slow pool gyre.

A blink of sun, a yell.

Arrow-swift, a blackbird strikes out in alarm call.

A body. A hairy body, legs raised, bum first, launches. *Phloosh!*

The green water surges and slaps, white and foamy and pure.

Spitting and spluttering, M shakes his head free of duckweed. Eyes tight, he wipes drool from his mouth, pulls water from his nose as apples rise and fall and bob around his beard. Together at the spout, the water drums a needle rhythm into skulls. No ears but theirs and no one to hear their voices as they settle in the thrum, face to face.

Below the surface they dip.

Ears – closed to the scrapes of land, to the feathers of air – hear only the dun-coloured song of fish and spawn. They leave the light above, hair floats like smoke, limbs push. The amber light and the fizz of sand and grit and bubbles roll against the bog brown bed.

Leaves brush hands, soft on ribs and chest and shoulders and thighs. A held breath pulses and pushes at heartbeats. In gold they tip and tumble further into the deep, circling and slipping, fast as fish, mouthing silver spheres and snaking with the flow, turning with the current.

They surface.

Water rills and splashes from goosebumps and sheened hair, laughing and teetering, rock to rock, grit and mud and leaf-stuck.

Sheep-cropped grass prints pink on white bodies as the sun soothes and warms to unknot the puckering chill in gulps of breath and shivers. A comfortable weary ache.

As simple as an apple falling from a branch, they kiss.

In shame they pick up scattered clothes. Eyes scan the fields. Birds watch. Trees witness. Bracken and stones torment a clumsy wardrobe and the water flows from the gathered pool to begin its faster descent to the lowest point of the village, back into the dark.

The part of them that so recently floated, drifted, is dammed. A heaviness, a plodding. It grew, solid and still and pushed into the earth, driven down by gravity, by a weight of sadness and dense flesh that wants to fall, to sink and hide in the mud below.

Display

It is night. A long day of work leaves them both weary. Hollow, tired of people and performing.

They sit side by side, in the dark, in the chairs at the front of the shop. The village outside is quiet under streetlights. Occasional footsteps carry on the evening air. Lone heels click, shuffle. Elastic groups of boys head to the station. Mist spreads the orange light. A blanket over them all.

Heat moves in the air between their bodies, radiating from aching shoulders and torsos and calves that almost touch. They stare forward, together. Stare out at the street, through the labels and signs on the door and the stacked paint cans and hanging displays. Sober, unadorned piles of stock.

Everything is ready for the next day and they find themselves quiet and sat. And they stay, with no energy for the stairs.

A shadow moves and a man stops outside, swaying. They know him, on his way home. They sit still, unseen, and watch as he looks at the display. He leans heavily on the glass with his forehead and closes his eyes a moment before turning away.

A grease smear to clean in the morning catches the light. They stare at the counter, at the shop and its thousands of component parts and lists of tasks and items, prices, packaging and pennies. It's their mooring. It holds them here and allows them what they have upstairs. Imperfect. Compromised but content.

Hands come together and grip softly. Warm, worn, hidden by night. They both rise and move toward the stairs.

Ring

Too much sun, M thinks. Not enough beer, B says.

They sit on their patch of rock, and talk and wait and watch. Hand holding hand holding hand. But the tightness around M's head won't loosen its grip. Too much sun, he thinks. A headache shimmer blooms and falls where the light reaches in. He shades his eyes.

They look at their wristwatches and the countdown toward the eclipse, a silver sprung-click, the synchronised red-needle sweep.

Light dims. Sheep settle, chewing. Patient. Skylarks drop from the sky into cover, as from a predator. It is neither the day they are in nor the night they left.

A piece of card with a careful pinhole. A camera, plastic and clumsy. Hairs tickle M's neck as he squints through the viewfinder at the small crescent, floating with ragged cloud in the palm of the other. The sliver diminishes.

Purple silence.

A breath held between them in the universal slow blink.
Heads push together.

A corona, a bright ring of light,
and a false dawn of cautious bird calls.

Cock-a-doodle

A cockerel; synthesised, digital. Each morning, its electronic voice slurs the time over and over until a hand hits the top of the plastic pyramid. It's a gimmick from the market, a joke, from M.

B remembers his dad's clock alarm bell, wound and unwound again and again. Ringing through the house, unrelenting until the mechanism slowed and it dulled. He wonders who has it now.

He rolls into the still-warm dip next to him where body heat lingers to call him back to sleep. Grateful for his regular Sunday late start.

No. I'll go, you stay there, lazy bugger.

B thinks of the farm cockerel, when there was one, hoarsely rehearsing a chorus ahead of the slow-light blackbird territorial call, before the shuffled cooing of pigeons in their loft at the old house. Dad with his own dad holding the racing birds like babies. The dads' heads together, backs turned, ringing a pink foot and placing the bird carefully back. As a boy he watched them both, from the top of the steps. The end of their line, their genetic full stop.

On and off, the cockerel clock marks the electric minutes of drowse.

In half-dreams he stacks up the multiples. The drawling cock-crow at nine minutes past, eighteen. Repeating loops count down the inevitable cold dash to get dressed for the day. He opens his eyes to the world at cock-a-doodle twenty-seven. Light blue the skylight above. Springs' dull *prung* sound on hollow floorboards muffled by dusty carpet. He curls back into their mattress on the floor.

He feels the stirring in the pit of his stomach and flexes and stretches, remembering the man who burns hot as a furnace next to him each night, and rolls back into sleep.

Kin

The shop phone rings.

Sleep-heavy, the bed is soft and B still doesn't move. It rings off. When it rings again, he starts from drowsiness.

Insistent, shrill, he stops it short. A dash downstairs. Out of breath.

Good morning, Jones and Son—

The voice is efficient. Impatient. The voice asks for Mrs Jones. Cold air. A shudder. Warmth sinks from his feet into the icy lino. Hairs rise and he's alert.

There is no Mrs Jones. Only Mr.

He looks at the receiver, confused. At the cradle and the dial. The shop-phone voice sounds distant, it needs to locate the next of kin. Who am I speaking to?

A large black fly climbs the window.

Kin?

A papery buzz beats against the glass.

Kin. Loaded with noise and meaning, too small – *kin.* The word sounds wrong.

He stares out.

Early this morning. Found by a couple walking their dogs. The van pulled up on the verge, engine still running. A suspected aneurysm. Alone, the shop phone says. We need a formal identification. Are you a relative?

No.

The fly skeeters on the smooth surface and falls into the display.

The shop-phone voice makes noise. The words don't connect.

Found.

The words are too small.

He pictures the windscreen of the van, still steamed with breath. He feels the leather seat beneath him and breathes in diesel and mud and looks through the misty glass at the view up to the rock. The moon blotting out the sun. He feels his hand in the warmth of M's hand and stares at his palm now, open on the counter.

The upturned body of the fly – tired with effort – spirals in a whirr of wings.

It all stops.

The last day of trade. Arrangements are put in place.

Customers shake their heads, solemn, familiar faces. Mam fusses. He wears a flat smile – *need a new job*. Performing grits his eyes, he gets rid.

He has his own black tie. He knows he has. He bought it for Dad's funeral. Before then the boys shared one tie for years, suddenly not enough for so many necks at once. He hasn't seen it since. Why would he? Did he lend it?

He finds it rolled up in a pocket. Moths have taken out the lining but the front is okay. He tucks it into his collar. In the small shaving mirror, he watches his hands try to knot it. He can't. His fingers feel too big. His shirt too tight. His trousers too short. The day too heavy.

A deep void opens and he stands next to it, at the edges. He wasn't there – *alone*. Why wasn't he there?

The family show up at the shop. A black car that smells of plasticine and shoe leather when the doors open. D*A*D in white chrysanthemums. Like a fairground ride. Lit up. Showy. He stands back. He daren't lay flowers.

Unfamiliar Joneses surface in the wake. They leave legal papers to read and sign. They ask little, they don't really see him.

The daughter is nice. He avoids her.

He wonders what she knows.

Grief is not kind when it finds him alone again.

It kicks his feet away; makes him retch. It hides in familiar handwriting on envelopes and bills. It cuts on spiked receipts. It burns his eyes of tears and clutches his gasping throat like a bully.

A giant ape devouring everything they had. Sightless, unreal.

M's hand fills the margins of the ledger. Lines run through the small writing caught in a grid made for numbers. Daily crossword anagrams. Doodles and phone numbers. News stories each month. Their time crossed out, in-between things.

He rests his own hand where M held the pen and follows the lines, even through the years, all the years, before he knew him. ~~B.1987. Snow. deep snow. Cut off. Kinnock lost. Salmonella. Eggs. Get eggs. Beat Eng6Nations. Princ Dai opens AIDS ward. Poll Tax, riots in Ely. Freddie Mercury.~~

~~Seer evicts ive Secret Secretive~~

No shop bell, no customers, no orders. The van returned, towed. Stock is sold as a job lot. The left-behind, unwanted goods still scatter the room, archaic rubbish thrown high in a flood. Sealing wax. Carbon paper. Fuse wire and real-flame-flicker bulbs. Walls, floors and shelves are scruffy. The cat strays. Noise stops. Fluorescent stars and circles – random, gaudy. Traces of displays layer, scar and stain. Pinholes. Blu Tack, Sellotape on dog-eared signs, prices and offers.

The sign overhead is reversed. Beneath it a previous font, the one before, a layer of paint over the one before that. Jones after Jones. He unscrews it from its seat, turns it upside down; code for a business closed. He turns every sign he finds. An ending.

He empties shelves. Whites out the window. A veil to the street.

The bed is cold.

With eyes closed he brings him back to his side.

He pushes himself down. He feels left behind. Extra. He lies lower and stays hidden, his hand rests in his pants. He drags M's clothes to the bed. He smells them and piles them over his body. He feels hollow, the weight is comfort. He looks for the wear on each cuff. M's neat repairs. A stain. He buries himself in fabric, coats and jumpers. He sucks at frayed edges.

He holds a button in his mouth.

His eye pulses and the world dances at the edges.

He notices the hairs on his knuckles. They feel alien, somebody else's.

He has no lines to speak. No directions, or invitations, or surprises. No new stories, the stage set is flat. His own voice stops abruptly, with no ear to hear it. He doesn't know what he feels – *natural causes* – he feels nothing that he recognises.

He tries to bring him back.

In his silences he hears footsteps.

He leans his cheek tight against the hardboard panelled wall until it pushes at his eyes and he breathes and licks. The bannister gloss sheens where their fingers once trailed and gripped.

The skylight is too bright in the gloom. Solid, heavy light. He's icy. He imagines warmth still there in the place they slept together unseen. Them alone, there alone. *Natural causes.* His smell. Aftershave lingers on sheets, rising fragrant on the heat of his body. He gets hard. He pictures a face close to his own, imagines the body that even now brings him to climax.

He doesn't move. Cold air finds the wet. Neither of them moves, neither of them speaks any more.

Three years is all. Barely much.

Dead flies gather, motionless on the sill. No whirr now from their wings.

He's alone, walking through and around the shop, hidden from the street. His feet won't rest, they plod up and down the steps, pausing at one end or the other, and he's puzzled whenever the rhythm of moving stops – *unnatural, natural. Unnatural*. One to the other and back. Something is gone, always just beyond where he treads.

A month passes. Staring, blank and unfocused. The world outside the shop is apart, separate. It is moving past him, moving away.

He searches everywhere, through everything. He wants people to know that they're not liars. That he is not a liar. He looks for anything M hid. Anything that would betray them. It's his ministry, his.

He removes the things that he must, bundles them up.

He climbs the hill.

Climbs back to their first meeting as the year turns. The place that lost its name, with no one alive to remember and no maps to mark it. Scarred with fly-tipping, the dump, the edge. Nowhere. The neglected place for lost boys. On its side a dumped Christmas tree glints with abandoned, half-stripped decorations, scraps of tinsel.

He sits where they sat. The sky starts to grey. Far below, a train lights up the curve of the track. He watches it glide south, escape silently away.

In the distance a dog barks deep, hollow.

He sparks the lighter. Warms it in his hands. The evening darkens around the bright flame. He turns the bundle until it catches.

Fire spits green and reaches his fingers and he drops it into the browned branches. The crackle grows to a roar and smoke pushes higher above red flames. It is a blaze, terrible and hysterical. The air melts and the hill quivers beyond, a shaky horizon. Heat sears his face and his back feels like ice. A bauble pops like a soap bubble. Sparks rise and the charred trunk smokes into the night air and he is alone on the platform of rock at the highest point.

He didn't burn them to protect himself, or to spare them both.

He burned them because they were not enough.

Fittings and fixtures throughout are of negligible value. Evidence of woodworm and rot in shelving to the rear of the retail area, the stockroom and outbuildings. We recommend this is removed and destroyed with immediate effect to prevent further damage. Lighting and electrical items in use, including but not limited to the electric heaters, till systems and alarm, are still powered but ineffective. To be disconnected and made safe, or disposed of by a qualified electrician and wiring stripped and updated.

Remaindered stock is not of good quality. A number of items have no resale value but may raise minimal funds at auction. We recommend boxed unopened stock, hand tools and farm equipment to be offered directly to Sallis & Sons (Hanbury Road), as a single lot. Costed per-item, or packaged sold-as-seen for a fixed sum and quick sale.

Living quarters to the first floor are basic. One sizeable bed-sitting room, one storage room and a toilet.

Furniture, functional but outdated. A key holder remains in the property for security reasons until his tenure expires following a 28-day notice period.

The street is empty.

The shop-door of home bells to the still-early-morning air. Three security locks meet, the key strike grates where the door warps, stubborn – a *clunk* of the barrel, a tumble, a turn. A dog barks at the distant diesel rattle of the first train.

Day breaks.

For the last time, he leaves.

Keys drop, slip and clatter, metallic on the brown mat that once gathered street grit, umbrella drips and the hinge-side nightly seep of dog piss.

He is locked out.

He found so little to take with him. The watch, aftershave. A Polaroid of the eclipse. He tries to hold their time together in the image.

In the small square picture his palm is outstretched, cupped. He holds the pinhole card and M clicks the shutter. He feels where M's head rests against his, watching ragged clouds curl apart.

And there he finds it, the faintest image of a crescent, a ring of light on his hand.

Acknowledgements

Thanks always to Tomos. And to Brennig Davies, Gwenllian Ellis, Francesca Reece, Stuart Fallon, Jon Doyle, Elaine Canning, Emma Geliot, Rosy Adams and Patrick for being early readers; to Literature Wales for their support and encouragement; to Cathryn Summerhayes & also to Laura at Granta for taking such care.

Thanks to Cynan, for guidance, and letting me make and find my own mistakes.

And to T and P, we ran together.

Keep in touch with
Granta Books:

Visit granta.com to discover more.

GRANTA